For the Love of Water

a collection of poetry and prose

Cover art by Picccola Arte

Written by Allie Iliana Herrera

For a long time, I've dreamt of waves crashing down on me. The ocean would swallow me whole. As violent as it is, I imagine this is what love feels like. It is what life is like. It is scary, but it envelops every inch of you all at once. You must continue moving anyhow. To hold your breath and dive, you must first learn how to breathe so that your chest fully expands. You must learn to breathe so you can move through love, fear, grief, and anger.

Allie

Growing Wings

Of The Void

¿Hija, pero qué haces?

¡Secate, secate!

I stand doused and embarrassed
in the kitchen light, my clothes sticky with cold
as my mother drapes the towel around me.
The ceramic bowl I had held until it overflowed
rests in my hands, while the mahogany chair
I had climbed in my backyard wrinkles
like paper in the rain, the top layer curling
where my dog had gnawed at it.
My chancletas soil the tiles with blots
so I step out of them, teeter barefoot
to my room trying not to splatter out the sides.
When again she asks, I tell her I am growing wings
like Pegasus, born from the quarrelsome sea
in storm and immune to thunderbolts.
I've danced in the showers of eight spring seasons
and when I learned that color reflects
in the void of raindrops,
I thought of my mother and her prayers
for me before school every morning.
Padre nuestro

que estás en los cielos.

By the window, I drop a smooth pebble
over the bowl, pray to the Universe
as it makes a splash and sinks to the bottom.
Padre nuestro

que estás en los cielos.

Head on my pillow, I wonder
if I would still be human when I wake

or become a fairy or a dragon or an angel
as I am lulled to sleep by the drumming
of the fat raindrops on the roof.

Conversations with the Buoy

The water is calm this day
inviting me to swim out.
There are no nets
just an inlet to the sea
from where you can see the A train.
I love this little beach
on this little park
just before the channel

the tongue of the Rockaways.
Here there is concrete
there is playground
there is sand
there is a patch of grass
gated for dog runs.
If I did not need as much as I do
I would sit at the shore

embracing my knees
my toes digging into that peace.
I would chat with the lone buoy
tethered to that spot
letting unsuspecting swimmers
know of sudden currents
that drag you under.
The buoy can tell me

how the crucifix tombstone
came to be placed at the sea side,
knows the fishers and oyster farmers
creeping the banks at sundown
when people in love saunter

and whisper sweet songs
has watched the children play
in the sandbox and the sticks

that were fetched by the dogs.
The buoy bobs the waves
better than any surfer I know
and should I ever decide
one day to swim off fifty yards
in the direction of the sea,
I will stop at the buoy
to contemplate the park's

corridors before swimming
back to the tideline
where the warm sand
is waiting for me.

Like the Fog

I want to be like the fog,
a cloud in need of rest,
draping its mantels of mist
over cliffsides and summits,
dissolving landscapes like salt
in Loja's repe, the green banana
soup comprising an entire
region's gastronomy.
I want to be like the fog
that gives the morning
a surreal tint, want to be
your first inhale of the outdoors
when you open the windows,
the breath that extends your chest,
travels down your windpipe, and curls
into your lungs like the smoke
of a recently extinguished candle.
I want to divert the reverberations
of sound and dampen noise
like fiberglass, give the illusion
of a muffled world where you
can hear yourself behold another day.
I want to scatter light
by the molecules of my being
and I want to polarize the glares
until everything is grey,
forcing you to remember
what was there, forcing you
to imagine what will be
once the fog dissipates
and steadily rolls
into the sequoia forests

where the leaves of ferns and cacti
will cradle the droplets.

The Art of Ripples

You can see how water is alive
by the ripples on the pond surface
when a rock is thrown in, the force
producing rings of peaks and troughs,
carrying the message of this disturbance.
The water, in its enthusiasm, will splash
together at the point of impact
to cover the dent the rock had left
and the ripples, with its crowd of molecules
in an uproar, will begin to lose momentum
until the pond surface is serene again
and the striders can continue their strolls
and the dragonflies can nest their young
and you can again see your own reflection
staring back at you from where the rock
had landed. You stay there a while longer
before making your way back home.

Icarus

Everyone knows the tale of Icarus
who wanted to fly to heaven.
He flew closer and closer to the sun
until the beeswax of his wings melted
and the feathers fell off one by one.
Icarus plunged into the sea
from this remarkable altitude
and hit the water as hard as concrete.
It happened silently—
the vegetable merchants did not notice
and the fishermen gathered the feathers
only after Icarus had drowned.
It was his father, Daedalus,
who found his body washed ashore
and named the nearby island Icaria.
Most think of the hubris
but I think of Icarus laughing as he fell,
having flown closer to the sun
than any mortal had ever been before,
and the cry of his father's name
when the cold water shocked Icarus
out of the perfect daydream.

The Earth Swallows Our Colored Pencil Drawings

The Earth has a way of swallowing things up
collecting things by the skin of her teeth
                                        so we don't notice
and although we may not at first
we will eventually feel   the absence
of that beloved notebook bracelet trinket box
an empty space
under the bed
where a stuffed animal lived in darkness
or in the cupboard
where your favorite mug collected dust
or that missing sock
whirlpooled into some other place.
It has just disappeared
and I'm not talking about the keys
or remote control you find
only when you stop looking—
        those are the brownies and pixies
                                and duendes
playing a trick on you.
No, the Earth swallows up what she wants
and disgorges them into another dimension
far   far   far   away
to dispose of the evidence.
I don't know why she does this
but I like to think she's like an elementary
school teacher that collects the students'
drawings cut-outs dioramas
and smiles when admiring them.

Backyard Berries

Every summer, the mulberries from my neighbor's mulberry tree would steadily fall from its branches and thud off the back porch awning. When nightfall invited cooler air, Mamá and I would sweep up the berries into a trash bag and throw them away, but by morning, there'd be enough of them to make wine again and we'd emerge from our bedrooms covered in mosquito bites. Dad made sure we wiped Nana's and Chichi's paws whenever they went out into the backyard and that we slipped out of our shoes before coming inside so we wouldn't stain the floors he mopped.

We did enjoy the sparrows, the morning doves, and the common starlings that visited us for their fill. During our meals, seated at the dining table, we'd watch them from the living room window. Sometimes, I'd go to Mamá's bedroom just so I could reach out her window to touch the mulberry tree's leaves with my hand.

Then, one summer, tired of the sweeping, Mamá spoke with the neighbors about the garbage flies in our backyard, the impossibility of going into the garage without stepping on some mulberries and making a mess. Within the week, the tree had been trimmed so that the longest branches no longer tapped Mamá's bedroom window when the wind whistled through. Still the berries fell and the birds chirruped. I was overjoyed that this part of my life had not changed, but was worried Mamá would want to speak with the neighbors again.

My tía came to visit one day. She too liked the birds and didn't mind the sweeping. "Dios santo," she said when looking into our backyard for the first time. "¡Qué re-galo!" My tía took an old bedsheet from the closet and a bucket into the backyard. She tied the corners of the sheet onto the steps' handrails and placed the bucket at the end of this makeshift trampoline.

"We will have enough
in the morning for pancakes,"
she said to Mamá.

Shipwreck and an Hourglass

Parallels are drawn from circles,
sketched with an unsteady hand.
I live in a centrifugal state,
propelled inward by a helix
invisible to the eye.

Alongside the ample lines,
I stretch for the sun.
My muscles elongate.
I tell an ugly honest truth,
but I am happy.

The circles turn into ovals,
then taper into ends like a tear.
They thin into silt, are carried away
by the wind, inching their way
into my most intimate parts.

My footsteps wend slowly
by the footsteps I hear behind me.
I am chased by moments of vestige,
a fear of rust and thirst,
and the need to get along.

Parallels are drawn from circles
with graphite and a shaky hand.
I live in a centrifugal state.
My feet are stuck
in the long shire drift.

There are stairs in lighthouses
spiraling for eternity, a window

overlooking the precipice. Let me
fall again and again to awaken
from a wet and sluggish dream.

Life Below as it Cracks

It's always a wave
          coming down like the roof of a mouth
finding my house of caña
                 the paper boat   or me
                 just me barefoot at the beach
I was terrified of the tide's return for so long
that I nestled into my nook
made myself a nest of nebulous silhouettes
reading of boreal forests and taiga
                 of people who traversed them
I've since pressed my ear against the contour
          of a conch shell
heard the gales of ocean currents flutter through
                      by way of wind
and now   I dream of a prolonged winter
to walk on the frozen surface
          press my ear against the ice
                 hear the life below it as it cracks.

The Law of Heat

There is no such thing as increasing cold
                        only the loss of heat
that causes molecules to slow down
like tiny rocks chipped from a meteorite
        floating through space
                        huddled together.
They do not even shiver.
It is only when heat returns that they move
                faster and faster until
                they let go
and water becomes vapor
becomes steam
becomes clouds
is becoming translucent
                                until transparent.

It is why my legs ache at night
in those summer days
when my body is not regulated to sleep
in spite of my efforts to keep the light
with Chinese lanterns
        hanging from the ceiling
                a phosphorescent moon
                        and lambent plastic stars
why rest comes to me in winter
        the blur of my frame decelerating
until I can make out my legs and my arms
        until I am as peaceful as a rock.

While Inside a Cathedral with an Arched Ceiling

I think about transforming
into a speck of dust shared among
our collective breathing
recycled between trees
and mouths and noses.
I feel my skin igniting as my blood boils,
the steam finding escape through my pores.
I am ready to combust
like the sudden bursts of confetti
littering the streets of New York City
on New Year's Day— nothing new
except I am now a year older
and maybe, if I'm lucky, a year wiser.
I think about dispersing
hoping then the earth will take me back,
and if not the earth, the wind,
and if not the wind, the sea.

A Lone Canoe in the Living Room

I like the gentle rain drops that collect
sparsely in the threads of my hair,
drops that tap my umbrella like a metronome,
drops that bring out the petrichor in the soil,
the inspiration of many leisurely walks.
I like the rain that pours angrily
as if the floodgates of heaven itself have opened,
the way it falls in glops and floods
the streets while I watch from my window.
The storms will only get worse
as the machine continues its profiteering,
that unscrupulous engineer of climate change.
It will become more perilous for passage
and for the people sheltered under scaffolding
and when the rain pours, I think of the day
when the rain will not stop and the oceans
brim over with their whales and sharks.
The shorelines will be encroached on,
that in-between completely erased.
We will be faced with Earth's cataclysm,
the way she has been seen as less than
her own creations formed after the first microbe
fed on the carbon compounds of her early waters.
I think of this and think I should buy
a canoe on Facebook Marketplace
and use it as a coffee table until it is time.

When I've Grown Tired

When my feet have led me to an unfamiliar place
and I've grown tired of searching
            before home reels me in with its fishing line
I return to that place where my existence
                              is not questioned.
I cannot deny the comfort of mud
                        as my feet sink closer
                              to Earth's mantle
or the pinkness of black raspberry brambles
at the end of winter   those sunny days
or the season's first turtle sighting
from over the bridge where one can see the ducks too.
They have returned   all of them
as if sprinkled onto the cascade's feet
                        by some majestic hand
to awaken spring from its slumber.
It is the only quiet I can stay quiet in
without feeling like the day has gone to waste
and when I remember this
                        I remember
                              the fishing line
that little gleam of string leading me back home
where there is always more to be done.
I will cut it eventually.

Lo Real Maravilloso

I used to cover my mirrors at night
with the extra bedsheets
stored in the closet.
If they can see me sleeping
from where they are,
peering patiently into my bedroom,
they will step onto my side
and take me away.
I covered my reflection
like this for a long time,
my body the collateral damage
of my desire to remain hidden.
I am just now synchronizing
with the face staring back at me,
                              my face.
I would love to be like water,
that meandering looking glass,
                    as it seeps into crevices,
capable of engulfing
entire frigates whole.

Pressed

The petals are falling
and I catch them quickly
in between a napkin,
place the napkin in between
the pages of a book.
I cannot bear the thought
of the world losing
any more color
despite the science
of falling leaves
in autumn
or the greying of hair
as we age.

The Last of Daylight

If you look at the sky in its last hours of daylight,
you might see a murmuration of starlings
weaving through ghost clouds at sunset
and you might see any figure you'd like,
determined by your conclusive mind,
a face, the number four, wrestling dogs,
or maybe even an omen of tomorrow.
You may even think that this is what a swarm
of bees must look like before the sting
and aware of these chimney smoke simulacrums
are the starlings, driving to the ground,
soaring before impact. Their feathers are aglow
in ultraviolet light, but us spectators only see
dull metal. This show is not for us,
as much as we may want it to be.
It is for the other starlings in-flight,
an invitation to their nightly roost
for once dusk falls, the murmuration
settles into their sleeping grounds,
each starling swaddled by the warmth of the flock.

When Everything is Green

My heart explodes at the sight of green
and covers most everything else.
Bits of it encase my lungs and diaphragm.
There are splotches on my spleen.
It starts as excited trepidation
and manifests in strawberry skin.
My smile sprawls wide with the thought
that all I need is a little chlorophyll and sun
somewhere along the forest floor
and I'd become part of the foliage.
Today is the day I will finally get there
dressed in my knitted pajamas,
and I'll root in place until only the fabric
of my imploded heart is left.

Before Cleaning on a Machala Morning

Bathed, she stands bare, folding her towel
in front of the curtainless window
four stories high.
People trudge to the train station,
commuting from and to their libation,
and women are adorned with perfume.
She cannot smell the aroma
but knows that it must be a collision
for the nostrils when black garbage bags
are piled by street trees,
engorged with the day-to-day use
of disposable everythings.
She robes herself, puts on her underwear,
and listens through the plywood bedroom wall
for her mother whose morning prayer
is the orbital spin of the Earth,
words thick with the weight of forgiveness
before the day has even started to clear space
for more of the unkind to be encountered.
She stands ironed with her ear against the wall
and recites with her mother,
relieved that there is no music yet
to wake the neighbors.
She walks barefoot into the kitchen
for a glass of water. Her mother will scold her.
The cold enters through your feet my daughter.
Quietly, she closes her door and slips
on a pair of pink fuzzy socks
and the oversized chancletas specific
to this weekly occasion. The water in the tub
has not yet drained and tiny chamomile rosettes
are still floating in the warmness of the bath.

The Science of Expansion

In my childhood,
I wanted to be a marine biologist
and would read books from the library
about all the different bodies of water.
I was obsessed with water molecules,
their two hydrogen atoms and one oxygen atom,
obsessed with water's shapelessness,
the way it becomes what contains it
until it overflows and swallows the container,
obsessed with the way my hair turned to seaweed
if I submerged myself underneath an incoming wave
at the beach, the way I'd squeeze my eyes tight
and wipe my face after popping up at the surface.
I was the water expert among my peers.
My sixth grade teacher once told the class
that ice is denser than water and I told him
that he was wrong, that water will trap air
as it freezes and the hydrogen bonds
will expand into crystalline structures.
That is why ice bobs like apples at a county fair,
it's how massive icebergs have stayed afloat
to become the cobblestones
of penguins and polar bears,
how entire ecosystems have survived winters
until the thawing of spring.

Photograph of My Family in Niagara Falls

I don't remember ever having gone to Niagara Falls.
All that I pretend to remember is the photograph
of my family and me in oversized blue plastic rain jack-
ets.
We're standing in front of a railing fastened
into the bedrock along the path leading you
to the plunge pool where the boat awaits.

People grip onto the handrail as they take little steps.
The cascade mist creates a fog over the gorge
that separates the blue sky so it is unattainable to us.
I doubt anyone has heard such a roar as that ravine.
Everyone is squinting. Everyone is laughing.
They are screaming.

As the boat unmoors and begins its slow loop
around the cyan pool, we all coil together on deck,
rocking with the ship, the closest many of us will be
to experiencing the middle of the ocean during a storm
without the actual threat of being gulped down.
My mother, she told me that I was not scared,

that I had leaned out as far as I could, my hand
reaching out into the air as if to collect the mist
in between my fingertips. Oh, how I had wished
my fingers were webbed! How I had wished to bring
some of that mist home with me, some of that roar,
some of that nervous laughter!

Making Out the Negatives

My mind is a camera reel
with the negatives wound up in a ball
somewhere in my mind's closet
and there's never enough time
to untangle the mess
and the ball has grown
to the size of my mind's living room.
Dishes left with crumbs
are stacked on the coffee table,
half-read books are shelved amid unfamiliar
name tags and photo albums.
I'll try to replay the movie still by still,
but all I see is black and all I hear is static.
No one believes me when I say
that I remember my baptism,
the black of the fountain's water basin,
that I kept my eyes wide open.
This is the single oldest memory I have
and this is what I see when I try
to remember anything else,
the gasp of air I take when springing up
after being underwater for so long.
I know I should use my dream journal
and do the work of opening doors,
using the stairs, looking through windows
even if I'm frightened that all there is to find
is a room full of clocks or a man
in a top hat dressed in all black
because I know that as long as I am frightened
of this ginormous memory reel ball,
I will keep on forgetting.

Beacon

The words "Welcome to the American Dream"
are scrawled into the peeling lackluster grey
of the fire tower's cab. I stand at the top,
quieted by the green of tree canopies and
the Hudson River winking under evening sun.
It is the moment amid the mess after devouring
what we love in a way that can only be deliberate
or the uncomfortable stillness after going forth
into the early mornings of incertitude
when you have yet to get your bearings.
I have been listening to the same ballad on repeat
where people clap and shake tambourines.
My heart has swelled with the violent
breaking of walls when I had meant to be gentle
        as I loved
                waited
                        and let go.
All that is left is the yearning to be still again
at the peak of a mountain
                or by a brook of jutting stone
but I'm beckoned by the current
to swim through the eddies and riptides
that guide me straight to the ocean's mouth.

Fever Dreams

I'm in a bubble
trying to stretch out my limbs in front of me.
This transparent sphere does not let my voice
escape
does not   it seems
let the color spectrum breach through
                all sonorous waves slamming
                        from one side to the other.
People peer in
                their bodies careening to where I am
and I think   thank goodness   someone sees me.
The surface feels like glass. I knock. I scream.
The people move their heads sideways
                curl a disobedient strand of hair
                        back behind the ear
        give a "Cheese" smile before leaving.
It's their reflection they see
                                not me
the bottom of a new pot before you wash it.
Why cannot I not pop this bubble?
Was it me who blew it?
Did I somehow fall asleep under my bed and entered
it?
It cannot just be water
that is trapped between the layers
                        must be more than soap
and if I did blow it
the bubble made from the waste of my breath
my lungs having rejected everything else
why am I
                still breathing?

But what if I didn't blow it?
What if the bubble was formed
                    in concurrence
between the windchimes and the wind
their sounds the ghost of a presence I cannot see
                    but that is there   as real
          as the warmth I feel at daybreak
and by thinking of that sun
                    that gives seedlings their fortitude
to flourish toward the sky
the bubble begins to warm and I begin to sweat
as if I had a fever   the kind that causes visions
and I think the bubble is sweating too
                    it is leaking   until it is not
          until it is melting onto the grass
making mud
          and I land on it
nearly skidding a fall.
I blink. It is the only reaction I could have
for no one could see me just a second before
would not react to my hysteria.
Instead   I unzip my sweater
let my skin come closer to being kissed
by the same rays that made the Sahara a desert.

Circles

Demons cannot hide in a place with no corners,
thieves cannot lie in wait of a wrong turn.
My fingers enjoy the contours of sweetness,
the ideal heart and the one beating in your chest,
all knuckles and fists, a snowball after the storm.

It is the shape of grace, intra-action sans the hyphen,
the returning love agleam in a new face,
the breeze that stands hair on skin,
a reminder that death is a transition like ash
to the brightest stars and that all our parents were once
children.

It is the shape of the moon that thickens and thins,
the omnipresent eye that watches us
when we think we are alone and blameless,
why our conscious weighs heavy like a rotting
field pumpkin picked at by the crows.

It is the shape of hunger and the solace of food,
the pollen center of flowers enticing bees,
the spiral of a shell belonging to an ammonite
preserved within the Earth's crust,
and therefore, reminiscent of home.

It is the dilation from when the first atom
collided with another atom and boom!
The Universe was born with all its spherical glories,
but we confuse time with the imminent threat
of a blade and cuts corners that will poke
our spleens and other organs.

The Parable of Sargassum

Small pebbles are in your shoes,
heavy as Jupiter. You think *never mind*
and continue walking with the laces in knots
that press against the bridge of your feet.
You walk past the neighborhood pub,
your favorite restaurant, the childhood playground,
past all the places your heart has grown fond of
until you reach the highway where the red taillights
of cars float like orbs against the darkening sky.
The highway thins out into a one-way street.
There are more houses than cars, more trees
than people, and soon, there is a dirt path
and no people at all. You hear bird calls,
pine cones dropping from their branches, the wind
rustling canopy leaves, and a river clamoring
with the urgency of hail breaking through
a windshield. You see a bridge
and decide to cross it. The wood slabs creak
under your weight and you remember the pebbles
lodged in your shoes. Finally, you undo the laces
and remove your socks to find the pebbles
have sprouted and your feet have overgrown
and become callused from constant friction.
You think, *Ah, yes, there is no need for this anymore,
the love, the anger, the sadness, the memories*
and you toss the pebbles, which were, in fact, bulbs,
into the river which leads into the ocean.
The river carries the bulbs like sargassum to join
all the other whispers history will never find
nor listen for and it scares you, for you are lighter
but empty and the green that surrounds you
is overcast with the shadows of trees and now

it is an abysmal black. You think,
Will I be forgotten too, the same way I chose to forget?
You jump into the river grasping for the growing bulbs,
but the ice on the mountain caps has melted;
it is early spring and the river has flooded.
The stones are glassy. The trees that have fallen
into the current are thin and break when you pull
yourself up so you swim in the direction of the flow.
It takes a while, but you reach the ocean's mouth,
and, too tired to swim, you instinctively float
along until you see a shoreline. It is unfamiliar,
but you swim towards it anyways, happy there is land.
You find the bulbs washed ashore with upright stalks
like celery. You go to collect them.
Yes, you think, *I am myself again. I am complete.*
You follow the trail into town and call it home,
build yourself a house on a plot of land and
leave enough space for a backyard. You plant
the bulbs here and each one, for there are four,
grows into a tree bearing different fruit:
apples, peaches, breadfruit, and figs.
Years later, you return to that same shoreline
and are reminded of the flying red taillight orbs
and the neighborhood pub, the sounds of gridlock
and construction. You are homesick now
so you make the trip to return if only for a visit.
On your way back to your old home, travelling on foot,
you find the bridge and your old pair of shoes
with stained socks scrunched inside. You try them on.
Your feet do not fit and you wonder
how they ever did in the first place.

Stains

If I'm quiet enough,
the walls of my room buzz in red
like the buzzing of a needle
on recently shaved skin
and I hear the whimpers—
they're not as loud,
eyes are open,
arm over the forehead for dramatic effect.
The second time around,
we grasp tightly onto the growing pains
that pervade lifetimes
like the Pleiades born from the ash
of the foodbearing tree or my mother's face,
how I learned to map her freckles and sunspots
only after she passed away.
I had a dream I owned a Cape Cod house
and my mother sat at a picnic table
in the meadow of my property.
She said, "Here, mija eat this green papaya.
Look, see the papaya trees?"
and I looked and there were many.
I like my fruits ripe enough
so they're just beginning to spoil,
a punto de podrirse, just enough
so when I take a bite,
juice spills out the corners of my mouth.
Don't let the hint of rot ruin the batch they say
and so I'm sure the vendors love me,
but I don't tell my mother that—
she already knows,
can smell the grapefruits
I keep at my desk until they're shriveled and dry.

Instead, I eat the papaya's pale flesh
that snaps off the way snow peas do.

Nectar

The Greener Grass

I've been a resident of this little town long before it even resembled one. You wouldn't believe what it was before the 2073 earthquake, wouldn't believe so many people once lived here. When the earth split open and the ocean flooded, the skyscrapers collapsed into themselves and the highways snapped like wires during a blizzard. I was only a girl then, still not accustomed to the city.

Only one major road leads into town now and it's constantly monitored. We get very few visitors if any and hardly any cars are registered to park within the parameters of this community. To be honest, I prefer this quaintness over the yelling and siren horns of a metropolis. I prefer these milk carton houses that share vining plants like wisteria over the apartment complex I had first moved into with my mother.

My home sits perched on a hill at the edge of Gennisi. It's a decent walk from the town center, but if you take Wharf Street all the way down, you'll find it. The front of my property is surrounded by a fence, but it isn't completely enclosed. Past my house is a grassy field dotted with dandelions that eventually blends into Cedar Forest. I know the forest well, but it's easy to get disoriented among the thickets of the underbrush if you aren't familiar.

My mailbox is a stone's throw from the base of the hill. "To the town's caretaker," the carrier says when handing me the mail and he'll proceed to catch me up on all the gossip he knows.

The earthquake that destroyed Gennisi City was one of many. The colliding tectonic plates triggered a series of tremors that disrupted Earth's magnetic field, altering the migratory patterns of birds and insects into colder regions. Health officials in white suits and gas masks made routine inspections for pests, eggs, and mosquitoes from the South and fumigated our homes with pesticides. Cases of vector-borne diseases surged and treatment was limited due to poor distribution of medicine across the nation. Many of my neighbors experienced organ failure to some degree. Most residents moved deeper into the country and away from the shoreline, and my mother gave many a tearful goodbye, but she never considered moving from this home she had learned to love.

"We came here for a better life and we got it, Millie," she'd say to me. "Now is our chance to give back."

My mother was a kind woman who took to teaching herself holistic medicine. She learned about all the limited natural resources provided to us and their properties. Though she had never studied this before, it came intuitively to her, something she would pass down to me. I often stayed home during this period of rebuilding because of illness, but my mother would put herself on the frontlines to help her neighbors.

The environment suffered. Crops failed to grow, flowers wilted prematurely, and weeds thrived. Pollinators were killed by invasive insects and their eggs were consumed. Our city became barren and inflation made food scarce. The Invasive Flora Act was enacted in 2075 to eliminate invasive species altogether, marking the beginning of Gennisi's recovery period. My mother and I sat on the veranda we built by the magnolia trees and celebrated with glasses of lemonade. She knew from what she learned that it couldn't stay this way, but it was a step.

From the hilltop, I watch the environmental aides go about their weekly duties. They wear wide-brimmed hats and forest vests detailed with a gold leaf emblem. Their tasks still include a thorough inspection of Gennisi's gardens to remove invasive insect larvae and invasive weeds growing in between the stones and park flowerbeds. The authorities are concerned that their resilience may outcompete the native flora, given their ability to withstand unpredictable weather.

The environmental aides wave when they see me at the hill and I happily return the gesture every time. It's been nearly sixty years and I have memorized the names of everyone who lives here. I particularly enjoy my conversations with my new neighbor, Favian Rivera, the son of Lilliana, who cycles over whenever the weather is nice. He often brings me baskets of food that I enjoy sharing with Jaime, my apprentice.

The first time he came around to see me, I recognized Favian from the local online newspaper, *Gennisi Life Daily*, that keeps the town informed about new residents, departures, and events at the town center— mostly children's plays and special-interest groups for adults that I would sometimes partake in. His family had probably learned about me through the same paper, which features phone numbers and brief descriptions of community figures on the last page. Mildred "Millie" Eyota is listed as a naturopathic caretaker. While Jaime, who updates my section with upcoming vaccines or outbreaks, prefers to call me a "doctor" or "healer," I don't identify as either.

Favian peddled over on his wooden bike. A woven basket was tied to the handlebar. He waved when he saw me standing by my mailbox.

"Hi, Millie," Favian said with a smile that looked exactly like the picture in *Gennisi Life Daily*. He had the same black hair smoothed over his head, thick eyebrows arched in the same inquisitive look I wore at his age. "I'm Favian. My family and I just moved here and my mother sends this basket to say hello."

There are no doctors in this town, but there are in the next town over which is a little bigger and under renovation. I am the next closest thing.

"Thank you, Favian. Please pass on my best wishes to your family," I said. I reached for the basket, but he kept a firm hold on it.

"Need a hand carrying the basket, Millie?" he offered, already dismounting from his bicycle. "I'm happy to assist you up the hill." He glanced up the slope and then at the gate that bordered it.

"No, dear. I can manage," I declined as he handed it over. "I might be old, but I still have some spirit in me." Inside was a loaf of sourdough bread from the newly opened Everyday Goods bakery near the town center. The marmalade was homemade and in a decorative jar.

"This looks delicious, Favian. Thank you again," I said. "How is your family?"

"We are well. Please do visit us sometime," he said.

Favian dropped off baked goods every Sunday afternoon and I became accustomed to waiting for him. On one such afternoon, when he didn't arrive, I went on ahead to the Greenmarket for groceries. Jaime was sitting at the kitchen table when I returned home.

"Did you manage to get everything we needed?" she inquires, walking over to assist with the paper bags.

Together, we place them on the table. "Yes, I got everything. They had a sale on tomatoes, so I bought a dozen. How does tomato soup sound for dinner?"

"That's perfect, Millie." Jaime quickly takes out the produce from the bags and places them on the kitchen counter before organizing them into the cupboards. She is biting her bottom lip, a sign that she has something on her mind.

"Jaime, what's wrong?" I inquire.

"It's about the Riveras. Aaron, the younger brother, is unwell. Favian arrived with Lilliana a little after you left. You couldn't sense that they were on their way?"

I ignore her question. It was not the time to be worrying about me. "What are his symptoms?" I ask.

"He has a fever and is itchy all over his arms. There's some swelling around his eyes too. It could be hives. Some diarrhea, but not that much."

"Do you think it's a stomach bug?" I stare at the rice-filled mason jar I'm holding before storing it in the cupboard.

"Yes, I've picked out the herbs already. They're hung out back, but—" she says, taking my hand and bringing me into the living room, "first, let's have a cup of tea. You're no good with a worried mind."

She walks back into the kitchen and turns off the stove.

This is my first visit to the Rivera family home. Sometimes, Jaime comes with me during these visits to help explain the medicine's effects and ingredients, but she stayed back to cook the tomato soup.

"You go on ahead, Millie," she said as I wrapped my pashmina around my shoulders. "I'll have a bowl ready for you when you get home."

With the taste of dandelion root tea still in my mouth, I headed over to the Rivera's. Aaron had been on the sofa, sweating his fever, a towel placed over his forehead. I gave him the remedy in a tea and monitored him for a while. Now, I am sitting at their living room table, observing Lilliana as she takes a slice of banana bread out of the microwave. Despite the late hour, she kindly offered me some for my journey back. The banana bread's delightful aroma fills the room and I anticipate savoring it soon with a cup of warm milk while chatting with Jaime about my time with Aaron. Meanwhile, Aaron rests snugly on the sofa, cocooned in blankets. Favian is at the foot of the sofa, reading.

"Can I get a slice for me too, Ma?" Aaron asks Lilliana. His cheeks still look warm, but the swelling around his eyes has subsided.

"You know you shouldn't eat anything after taking the medicine, mijo, and it is getting late," she responds and places the bread slices that are left into a cloth bag. As a precaution, everyone has taken a dose in capsule form, including myself, and I leave instructions on how to disinfect the house with a natural spray I provided.

Lilliana hands me a small container with my slices of banana bread inside. I stand from where I'm seated and thank her before turning my attention toward the end of the hall where Roberto has emerged.

"Hello, Millie," Roberto greets, stifling a yawn with his hand, a smile forming as he notices Lilliana's cheerful expression. "I'm guessing everything is alright with my son?"

"Yes, just a stomach bug. He'll be better soon," I assure him.

"Thank you, Millie." Roberto turns to Aaron. "Let's get you to bed."

"No, I want to talk to Millie!" Aaron shouts. He's got his voice back which is a good sign. I chuckle to myself.

Lilliana offers me an apologetic smile and places a comforting hand on my shoulder. I shake my head to indicate there's no need to apologize. I observe Roberto, whom I had only met once at the Greenmarket with the rest of the family, sitting on the sofa next to Aaron, squeezing his little toes. He is clad in plaid house pants and a black long-sleeve shirt, his short hair sticking out in various directions just like Favian when he rides his bike on a windy day.

"Why don't you get ready for bed?" I suggest to Lilliana who must have been by Araon's side the entire day and was not yet in her pajamas, "I'll speak with Aaron a bit longer, but only if he agrees to go to bed soon." I give Aaron a wink.

"Deal!" Aaron responds, playfully hushed by Lilliana. Mimicking her, he puts a finger to his lips and rolls his eyes when she looks away.

As Lilliana disappears into the bedroom and Roberto heads to the kitchen to pour himself a glass of water, I bring a chair over to the sofa to sit by Aaron. I notice that Favian has not moved and his eyes are fixed onto the current page.

"Millie, why don't you ever invite us to play? I want to explore over the hill!"

I place my hand on Aaron's forehead and breathe a sigh of relief when I realize the fever has indeed gone down. He didn't need to see a doctor after all.

"Am I really better?" he asks.

"Yes, you are, Aaron," I say. I smooth his honcy-brown hair. Lowering myself to his level, I whisper, "Would you like to explore the hill with me now?"

He nods, his gaze unwavering.

"I wish I could bring you, but it might not be a good idea," I explain. "The plants tend to get restless at night."

Aaron's eyes widen like moon pies and he remains silent for a moment before bursting into laughter. "You're silly, Millie!" he says. He's turning eight soon and

I wonder if my explanation will satisfy his curiosity like it does with the younger kids.

Meanwhile, Favian is still sitting at the end of the sofa, motionless, holding his breath.

"What are you reading, Favian?" I ask.

"Oh, I'm rereading this for school," he says. "I've got a report due on Thursday." He shows me the cover for *The Kingdom of this World* by Alejo Carpentier. It was a book I've also read. "I'm writing a thesis on it," he says.

Lilliana returns with a washed face and house slippers. "Thank you, Millie."

"I promise to have you boys over for a playdate one day," I tell them before bidding farewell. I hum to myself during the walk home, the cake still warm in my hands.

I had to produce a few more batches of the same remedy that week, including one for the potable water vendors, free of charge of course. Jaime alerted every household with instructions for disinfection, similar to the ones I had left at the Rivera home, and a reminder to boil all water before use.

"He's on his way, Millie," she informs me as I enter the living room, my eyes still sleepy. "Didn't you hear it?"

It was the music that roused me awake, the sounds of the flute and drum coming from Jaime's laptop. I sit beside her on the sofa and look through the window behind us. The sun bathes our green land, but has not yet reached the floor of our living room. Jamie turns off the music and closes her laptop.

"I haven't been feeling like myself," I admit after a brief silence. "I've been feeling weary."

Jaime turns to me. "Are you unwell?"

I gesture dismissively.

"Shall I fetch the basket?" she offers.

"No, dear," I decline. I touch her shoulder and give it a reassuring squeeze. "I'll go."

Jaime has been living with me for nearly a decade. I sensed her travelling to Gennisi on foot a day before her arrival and I made sure to wait for her by the town entrance. "It's my granddaughter," I told the guards so as not to raise suspicion. "She was looking for my house and got lost at Cedar."

When I could make out her silhouette on the road, I ran over to her. She dropped her bag as I did. "Granddaughter," I said, "I have been waiting for you!" I gave her a hug. "Play along. They will not let you in otherwise," I whispered into her ear.

"Grandma Millie?" she asked. "You look so different. I'm so happy to see you!"

So she had indeed been looking for me. Her presence was strong enough to slightly shift the air patterns around her and I noticed the birthmark in between her thumb and forefinger. It was shaped like a leaf, similar to mine.

Favian hands me a basket containing his mother's banana bread, a small pot of maple syrup, and eggs from a nearby farm.

"My mother sends her thanks for looking after Aaron," he says.

I smile as I accept it from him. "Please extend my gratitude to your family," I say. "I am here whenever they need me."

"Need help taking it over the hill?" Favian offers.

I inspect my grip on the basket handle, noticing the wrinkles smoothing out on the back of my hand. I recall my mother telling me that the number of moles on your body correlates to the number of times that you have been reincarnated and I remember the cheese in my hot coffee during this conversation, how much I loved to eat it when it stretched.

"No," I say after a while, "but thank you for asking. It's good to see you again."

"Are you okay, Millie?" Favian peers into my face, his eyes darting between the corners of my eyes. "You look tired."

"Yes, dear. I am okay. Take care of yourself," I say.

Favian nods and hops on his bike. "Okay, just had to make sure. See you later then!" he calls out as he rides away.

Jaime and I take enjoy exploring the gardens during our daily walks. When she hums, the flowers turn towards her. She possesses a unique benevolence towards plants, understanding their language well enough to communicate with them. I have never met anyone like that, but I knew of her capabilities the moment I saw her. She has quickly excelled in her apprenticeship and no longer needs my guidance on most tasks.

Jaime particularly adores the late spring bloomers that attract throngs of butterflies and bees. We eagerly awaited their return after the Act amidst concerns that a single enforced action wouldn't be able to resolve the situation. However, I ensured our pollinators came back.

While walking home with our arms linked, Jaime suddenly pauses.

"Millie?" she calls, uncertain.

"What is it?" I ask, but then a gust of wind hits me, and I sense someone at the base of the hill. "Who's there?"

"Favian," she murmurs. "It's Friday. What is he doing there?"

I grin at the overcast sky, slowing the pace of the walk. "He's just there thinking," I say. "He always offers to bring in the basket. He's curious is all."

"This isn't good," Jaime remarks. "What if he reveals everything? What will become of our field?"

"Trust me, Jaime. He'll understand."

✳✳✳

The humid air clings onto me and makes it hard to breathe as I stumble through the darkness.

"You're crazy, Favian," Josh remarks. "She just values her privacy and has likely lived here her whole life." He sits up from the bed and his eyes linger on my sneakers on the windowsill. "This is ridiculous."

"That's not entirely accurate," I counter, pulling on a black hoodie and ignoring his other comment.

"Is that so?"

"Yeah, she moved here when she was a bit younger than Aaron for the same reason my family did." I recall the Darién Gap and the terrible wait for help in constructing the bridges. Aaron was unwell, much like when Millie came to help, but there was no quick treatment available in the middle of the rainforest.

My family moved here a couple of months ago. We were already planning on relocating due to the state of the economy, but then periods of intense flooding occurred after periods of drought. It was one thing after the other and our governor would not admit that there was any kind of environmental crisis. That was it. We had to leave before escape was guaranteed death. It's a good thing we did. There's nothing left of the Gap.

Josh reclines on the bed and covers his eyes with his hands. "Don't tell me. You actually looked her up?"

"Josh, she's hiding something. I know she is. She never lets me help bring the basket in."

Approaching the window, I lift the mosquito net. I've only ever seen Millie angry during the town meetings with the Environmental Authorities and I am dreading facing her if I'm caught. But this was Millie, the woman who visited our home when Aaron had the stomach flu. The sight of a doctor in a white coat meant chemotherapy, needles, things nature couldn't cure. We turned to Millie for ailments that could be treated. She wouldn't be too upset.

"I'll return before sunrise. Please keep this between us," I whisper. "Don't tell my parents."

"Sure, man. I won't say a word," Josh assures. "Just stay safe."

Josh's house is nearest to the southern end of the town. The walk to the gate couldn't have been more than twenty minutes. Gradually, there were less houses lining the streets until the path to Millie's was surrounded by bits of stone and unkept grass. I only had a flashlight to guide me.

Passing Millie's mailbox, I make my way towards the gate. The moonlight illuminates the latch and chains securing the door. As I climb over, my black sweatpants snag on a small spike of the railhead. Was she simply seeking privacy? I had tried to envision something like the local farms with apple trees, strawberry fields, and ripe nectarines hanging from low branches. Perhaps Millie supplied most of the produce to the Greenmarket, or maybe she owned a lot of land, something that was frowned upon, and she wanted to keep her wealth a secret. Stepping forward in my oversized black hoodie, I move through the night with my shapeless silhouette. The quarter moon intermittently helps me see where I am going, casting light on her home at the top of the hill.

"Damn. It's a climb. Does Millie really not mind doing this every day?" I mutter to myself. Had she rejected my help all this time because she wanted to hide?

Getting closer to the house now, I see how modest it is, but the surrounding land is huge with a spacious veranda and two magnolia trees in the yard. It stretches all the way around Millie's house and I very carefully make my way to the backyard. I see glimpses of purple, blue, and yellow peek through what seem to be weeds. There aren't any trails, but I do see parts where the grass has been matted and split. This is probably the route Millie and Jaime take when collecting herbs. I just have to make sure it's herbs that I'm seeing. From where I am, it all looks like a tangled net.

The descent is swift, driven by gravity. I didn't think anyone would be awake, but I make out the outline of a figure peeking out from behind the teal curtain of the house when I look back.

"Shit," I whisper. I feel needles along my right calve as if my legs were not covered by the heavy fabric of my sweats. I am surrounded by thistles that I had not seen. Staring at my caught foot, I notice the sheen of dark red and black beetles moving onto my legs. I jump backwards, my foot entangling further, and I fall onto the moist soil.

"Get off of me," I say through clenched teeth, but each time I try to stand, I am pulled downwards towards the ground again. I swat a beetle on one on my pant legs and a milky substance oozes from it. I cough at the rancid smell. More beetles are appearing now. I look upwards and see Jaime leaning against the door frame with her arms crossed.

"Jaime! I'm sorry!" I shout, but she shushes me as she hurries over.

"Favian, you know you're not supposed to be here!" she hisses. I feel the grip around my ankle tighten like a tourniquet.

"Jaime," my voice cracks. "Millie!"

"Keep your voice down! Millie is—" Jaime takes a moment to return her gaze to the open door. There is now light pouring out onto the yard. "Awake, never mind, she's awake now.

Jaime and I continue looking at the front door in silence. Sweat is pouring down my neck. There's no one there. Did Jaime hear a loud thud? Did Millie fall from her bed? I hadn't heard anything.

When I do see Millie coming out into the backyard, she is in her white night gown and the long braids of her white hair are out. She is without her glasses and her face reminds me of the moon when it's full. I'm embarrassed to be where I am, seeing her this way.

"Jaime," Millie says and places a hand on her shoulder once she makes her way to us. Jaime turns to face me and smiles. I see the slight crookedness of her teeth, the freckles on the bridge of her nose. I realize then that I don't see her around too often.

"Fine," Jaime says and begins humming. The ground clears as Millie crouches next to me.

"Didn't I tell you the plants get restless, boy?" she half-scolds.

"You mentioned that to Aaron," I say. I grasp her outstretched hand and pull myself up. Jaime heads back to the house, leading the way with us trailing behind. I glance back at the spot where I had just been. It is now concealed with brambles, the plants having changed their place.

Once inside the house, I take in the snow-pea sofa and the dark wood coffee table. The biggest painting in the living room is of an eagle soaring over a maroon-red backdrop on the wall. A faint whitish gleam covers it. I wonder if Millie had brought it along when she relocated here.

There isn't a single ceiling light. Hanging plants drape over our heads like beaded curtains. The string of pearls is reaching toward the standing lamp on the corner.

"They move," I manage after sitting in silence, staring at the cup of tea Jaime had brought me. "How is that even possible?"

"Plants are intelligent species," Millie says, sitting across from me. Jaime settles beside her on the opposite sofa. "They've learned that they're not wanted and I let them know they're safe here. They've learned human danger, can you believe that?"

"No! Like—" I begin, but there aren't any words that can make me understand at the moment. "What if they spread?"

"Please drink some tea. It'll calm you from the fright," Millie says.

I look to Jaime who nods. "It's a blend I made. Chamomile and lavender." She takes a sip from her own cup held between her hands. "Sorry about scaring you, Favian."

"You should apologize for scaring me!" Millie exclaims to Jaime who looks like she's about to cough out her tea. Her eyes squint from holding in laughter. Millie then turns to me, laughing softly to herself. "Jaime wakes me up near midnight, 'Someone's coming,' she says. 'I think it's Favian.' I told her it probably was and to let me sleep."

"You knew?" I ask.

"We can sense these things," Jaime responds.

"It's illegal, what you're doing," I say. "You're breaking the law."

"You're trespassing. That's illegal too," Jaime retorts.

I look away, my face growing warm. Jaime is right. I am the intruder. That's why the weeds attacked me. Maybe I should have listened to Josh.

"Favian, I'm doing no such thing. They are aware." Millie puts down her cup. "Besides, what does the law know?" By "they," Millie meant the environmental aides who never inspect her home from what I've seen. She was probably referring to the local government, too.

"Why hasn't this spread into town?" I continue. "What would happen if—"

"Favian," Millie interrupts. "Favian, this little world has done great things for the one outside the gate," she says. "I can speak with them. My mother taught me how and now I'm teaching Jaime. As long as they are loved and happy here, they have agreed to stay within the boundary of the space I offer."

"But the bugs?" I ask.

"Have no reason to leave. They're also happy feasting here."

"Can you speak with them too?" I ask. I was trying to keep from laughing at my nervous incredulity. This was as real as the cuts on my ankles.

"No, but they're like the weeds, child. They know they are not protected past the gate. If they go past it, the environmental aides will spot them during their weekly rounds."

I eye the string of pearls to make sure it doesn't tap me on my shoulder.

"Jaime and I, we can feel things, auras. Everyone has them, though it also depends on the day. If Jaime had not woken me, I would have slept through the night." Millie laughs.

"That's what worries me," Jaime whispers.

"Why is this here?" I ask.

"To keep the town safe, at least to do so for as long as it can. It's been kept a secret so as not to stir panic. No one understands balance. They think something is bad and they want to kill all of it. That will do much more damage," Millie says.

"So the medicine, does that come from here too?"

"Yes, most are a blend," she replies, "of both weeds and herbs from the Greenmarket."

I nod and nestle back into the soft fabric of the sofa. I feel the glow of the room hugging me. The lamps are still on and the sky is a lighter shade too. I yawn.

"You should head home, Favian," Jaime starts.

I should head home, yes. Not home, but to Josh's place. Josh, who has probably fallen asleep again, waiting for me. I get up, but the foliage of the hanging plant above me falls onto my head. I immediately sit back down.

Millie chuckles. "Oh, they were the same way with Jaime too. Don't worry. This time, they'll let you cross."

But when I wake up, I am not at Josh's. I'm at my house and I don't remember exactly how I got there at first. It's during breakfast with my family that I remember the walk over, accompanied by both Millie and Jamie, and the field of weeds waving goodbye. I didn't tell anyone, not even Josh.

The rest of the summer was slow. I saw Millie every Sunday as per usual to drop off baked goods from my family's bakery, and Jaime waited for me most times too. They did invite my family over for dinner one night. I was giddy with the excitement of their secret, of knowing something that my family didn't. Millie didn't offer to show us the backyard and my parents didn't ask to see. Aaron was content playing on the porch swing Jaime had set up in between the magnolia trees just for him.

While my mother chatted with everyone and Aaron sat at the table listening, I withdrew and sat on the sofa next to the string of pearls.

"Hey," I whispered and a string coiled around my pinky finger.

I started college in the fall after that summer. My family wanted me to stay local, but I chose to go to Coral Springs University, several towns and an actual city over. I'm currently taking business courses, but one year in and my eyes are glazing over the textbook pages.

I have a recurring dream of my foot caught in the same thicket of roots, the bugs trailing up my legs and onto my chest, crawling onto my face and into my mouth. The smell of chamomile and lavender keeps me awake at night and I draw blueprints of a new Earth filled with cities and towns like Gennisi. The oceans are not as angry nowadays and flooding is slowly decreasing, a sign that another shift is underway.

I received a message from Jaime the other day along with the usual email from the family. "Come visit us this summer!" they both read. "Millie misses you," read Jaime's.

I plan to switch my major to environmental science next semester. As for the upcoming summer, I will visit. I'll see my parents, Aaron, Josh, Jaime, and Millie. I've been hearing whispers lately like a radio emitting static, telling me to go back home.

After the Fall

Breaking Bones

I.

I was the child soaked in rain
holding a bowl with outstretched hands
in the middle of a storm.
I had learned somewhere that growing wings
was to experience bones breaking,
to have the skin on my back stretched so thin,
it would rupture with feathers that smell
like the cinnamon of last holiday season
when my father had brought me to the ice rink
on my wobbly legs that buckled when tilted.
In between the parted curtains of my bedroom
window, moonbeams seeped through
alongside reckless faith, and spilled onto the bowl.
I repeated stringed words that fastened
my pulse onto the bed I laid in
and forced my eyes closed.
I dreamt of the blue stone at the bottom
of the bowl descending deeper
into it, through it, until it was in the ocean,
descending deeper still.

II.

The bowl remained on my windowsill
like a mantelpiece above a fireplace
and I lay dreaming of all the possibilities
until a wind embossed my bare arms
with goosebumps and woke me.
I was still drowsy but refused slumber,
and I left the house in shorts and a sweater

to sit on the curb across the street
from where I could vacantly stare
at the bowl's curvature until sunrise,
but cold air had traveled through
the threshold of my door.
My father did not need to open it
to know that I was missing.
He knew I was intolerant to temperature
drops from my bouts of insomnia.
"I need to grow wings, Dad," I cried
as he sat next to me, "I want to go far away."
He said, "You'll grow your wings one day, Ash.
What about some Taco Bell for today?"
and we ate triple layer nachos in the dark
with the TV on low volume.

III.

I eventually stopped checking for protrusions
on my back when changing in front of a mirror,
started carrying an umbrella when it rained
or just in case the forecasters were wrong.
Sometimes, I go to the roof to sit
underneath the moon with a pitcher of water.
Sometimes, I am alone and other times,
I am with someone else and we are smoking
weed, leaning our heads far out over
the building's edge. I tell myself I rather be sad
than angry, which is sadness anyways,
but much more respectable,
expelled by tears rather than blows
and does not burn like hot coal does.

Sometimes, I lay on my bed thinking this
and other times I catch air
by suspending myself in increments
and landing with bent knees.
I have more of a bounce
now that the bones of my legs
have grown denser with the fall.

Heart Like the Womb

I want a heart like the womb,
a passageway through which life enters this world,
a burgeoning cavern so that it makes space
for all the people who enter it.
I want a heart that remembers it is bleeding
all throughout my body all the time,
even when I'm sleeping.
I want a heart that holds my tongue
while it quietly incubates anger
so I may speak with understanding.

I am not all grace.
I trip over my words and time's patchwork,
but am blessed to know love,
to know that it tastes sweet and bitter
like sugar in my coffee on a fatigued morning,
that it resides in the curvatures of circles
and collects negative space for dawn.

I want a heart that loves this way,
like a solar eclipse emphasizing the lunar linings
of a jawline or the lobe of an ear,
a heart that can love the sketch before the painting,
can love the blank canvas before the sketch.

But to have a heart that stretches like the womb,
my innards must first rearrange themselves,
make me a foreigner to my own body.
I must first realize that I am bleeding
all the time and not be ashamed by this.

To have a heart like the womb

I will have to regurgitate all
that does not serve me,
head over the toilet bowl,
tears springing forth my red face,
to make room for new life
in this amniotic fluid I have created.

For the Love of Earth

Earth is the best mother,
keeping the climate as best she can
to sustain microscopic organisms
birthed when magma met the sea
and rose like the foam
from which Aphrodite was born.
The Earth loves by her gravity,
the sheer pull of her mass
that bends even spacetime.
Her water has flowed in perpetuity,
quenching dry mouths and cracked
soil alike, harboring entire vessels
of flesh and steel, and wintering skies
with snowflakes and ice.
Even our babies are born the wettest
they'll ever be, for we dry out
as we age like leaves left out in sun
for too long or like an old tree bark
whose roots must absorb water
quickly to reach all its rings.
Can you imagine if Earth
was like Enceladus, the sixth moon
of Saturn with subsurface oceans,
her organic matter dripping out
into space? Earth would continue
to empty until there is nothing left
but for solar wind to penetrate
the atmosphere and destroy
the radios, pipelines, and satellites,
nothing left but for the sun flares
to channel through our cities and villages,
drying us out until we burn

like powdered aluminum sparked
and we would drip out, too,
into space until tugged into the orbit
of another planet or sucked
into a black hole
from which nothing can escape.

The Alley Pond Giant

The oldest living thing
in New York City is a tulip tree
growing in Alley Pond Park.
It is four hundred years old
          old like the soil underneath
          that formed part of the glacial moraine
when the ice melted fifteen thousand years ago.
The park is serenity in the metropolis
where you can find kids filling
their water balloons at the fountain
and riding their scooters
          hear the bell chimes as they pass.
If you go deeper into the brush
crickets rubs their wings for music
and cicadas chirp their mating call.
If you go deeper still
          step off the path and down the hill
you will see how people
have chewed through the wire
of the fence like mice
and made a small lodging
for themselves at the trunk base
          where the poison ivy sprouts
to exchange geocaches and letters.
But can you imagine such a tree
                    more than a hundred thirty feet tall
                    and over eighteen feet in diameter
on the city streets where trees
are measured and spaced
to make room for human foot traffic
for what would the neighbors say of such a tree.

"The view of the building next door is obscured. We
should trim the branches, trim the trunk. What a mon-
strosity of a thing."

It is better that the Alley Pond Giant
is among its own family
          that we must follow a trail
                    until we cannot see the highway.
We do not know how to grow so tall
how to share so much space among our own.

Gemini

My flaw as the Gemini lies in the way I love.
Like wildfires
I consume the breaths
from mouths agape and sting the eyes
that don't water in the face of burning.
I am the air that kindles the flame
germinating seeds protected by tree wood.
I step too close
              like Icarus flying to the sun
                        and I laugh as he did.
My love is Venus with a mirror.
It is winged Ishtar who fills bellies
with grain and sharpens the sickle
in preparation for war.

My flaw as the Gemini lies in the way I evolve
from winter
        to spring
            to summer
                to fall,
shaking off ice from my winter coat
like snow caps before an avalanche
or brushing the beads of sweat
from my chest with sticky fingertips.

My flaw as the Gemini is the forked tongue
I was born with
              hiding behind my lips
but I have spent years grinding my teeth
against the edged lining of this flesh
to round out the syllables
and make softer words to form harbors

on which you can rest.

Perhaps this is why the flower
of the Gemini is lavender.
We are often in need of repose
often wanting to cradle others
between the halves of our selves
        to keep them warm
            trying not to lose heat in the process.

Perhaps this is why the constellation's
brightest stars
are Pollux and Castor
        the twins holding hands
            a shared immortality in death.
The Gemini weeps
with the saints and the sinners
        blossoms pink in winters frosted over
like the Japanese apricot tree
        both Hades and Olympus
            both Hades and Persephone.

Talking to Myself

My tía partakes in quiet confessions.
She converses with God nightly
and needs no one else as a witness
as she sighs at the stars from her bed.
She says that as long as her confessions
extend into compassion,
the karma of the world will upright itself.
She need not do anything else.

I do not go to confession once a year anymore
but I too enjoy the daily conversations
between myself and the blue sky.
In what ways have I failed to look after
my peace? In what ways have I not been gentle?
I remind myself that if I did my best
and could not do more, that it is okay.

In writing this poem and many others,
I have made my confessions public,
have shared the lurking sentiments
and incriminating questions.
It may be a desire to tell my story,
a way to relate to others and the world
and though I say I don't confess,
I guess I am confessing something today;
that I sometimes fail to steer the ship
as it crashes onto the rocks along the shore,
that I love talking about angels,
but believe our shadows must play
with light too. I confess the love I feel
for the devil in the details
and the framework of our cosmology.

Now, I believe in reincarnation,
that one lifetime isn't enough time
to learn all that we need to.
Atonement has already found me
in her black trench coat and green eyes,
bringing with her the consequences
of a previous lifetime's mistakes,
but in loving enough in this one
to pour into the next, I hope to be reborn,
surrounded by this same love.

The Vortex

Cosmically speaking
we are made of stardust
planets with our own orbit
and gravitational pull

Loves
I had no idea
by how little we have missed
each other in a past life
blocks away or a day apart
in the span of many years

have no idea how many times
we'll let go in this one

I was told that happiness
is a conscious choice
            but consciousness
        makes only five percent of our choices

Where does happiness reside
if not in the subconscious
        in the spiritual heart
        that can't seem to keep its eyes open

It cannot be mapped like the human brain
color-coded by a monitor
cannot be seen how we can now see
the inside of a human body
at an autopsy

No

I want to be happy
until I no longer question
my subconscious choice to be
like a crayfish emerging from the lake
                    to greet the moon

The Remedy of Most Problems

My heart stirs in the solitude
of being requited of a love only felt
alone among the discarded flowers
I've lined up along the bedroom sill.
I've salvaged them from the spoils
of ritual I love you's, I miss you's,
my greatest sympathies' professed
from the local compost bin.
I ruminate the colors before a dream
comes to tie my senses into a bouquet
and takes them away for further questioning.
The premature wilt of the flowers,
their stems cut at a forty-five degree angle,
reminds me of how beauty leaves the body
like the wet of dying cells,
reminds me of my cardboard resolve
to persist gently as a lamb
in the evening grass at dew point
when the air has soaked in the vapors
of the oceans and streams, lakes
and rivers, and can hold it no longer.

The Deep Belly of the Ocean: a poem about
the women in my life and I

The women in my life
must be gripped onto tightly
lest they should drift off into the deep belly
of the ocean, unanchored boats
on shores I'm unacquainted with
where purple starfish ward off hungry crabs.
They are the orange of tigers in tall savanna grass,
the black of olives found on trees
in Central America, the brown of clay
made from soil, sculpted into stoneware
and porcelain.

The women in my life
are the steam rising from my kettle
as I pour the boiling water over tea bags.
They are the steam from hot showers
that leaves a residue on the glass doors
where I write my morning reminders
and they are my breath in low temperatures
reminding me I am part dragon,
part fog, rolling into the city,
spreading like a blanket.

The women in my life and I
hold fervor in our stares.
We can't hide our hearts from you
even if we tried to. Our pupils
leap into the air like mirages
from heat waves when it seems as if light
is emanating from the ground.

The centripetal forces of our bodies
thrums through our guttural laughter,
is displayed by the teeth filling in our smiles
when we walk into a room.

Our love is an everlasting one.
In moments of stagnancy, we launch
each other into the mouth of Charybdis
if only to instill us with enough faith
to sail our ships despite Poseidon's wrath
and when we overcome the stumbling blocks,
our happiness is a shared one.

We are stubborn and self-directed,
following our separate trajectories,
overlapping every so often and when we do,
we grip onto each other tightly
lest we should drift off into the deep belly
of the ocean, following our own North star,
wherever it may take us now.

A Friday In Afterschool

There is flour all over the floor.
My footprints have created a trail
like a clue to the crime and the cafeteria
lunch tables are covered with paper
and the paper is covered with drawings
of princesses and swing sets.
Forty kindergartners and first-graders sit here,
their faces red from playing soccer at recess.
Bowls of flour with food dye are in front of them.
They have been looking forward to this Friday
all week after nonstop outdoor rehearsals.
for the Street Festival. "I'll know when you're ready for
water when I see your hands folded nicely like this,"
I tell them and demonstrate prayer hands
with the fingers interlocked.
Each student, backs slouched after a long school day,
sits straight like a cadet and no one whispers
a single word. *Very soon, just a bit longer,*
we will wait, they think loud enough for me to hear.
I look around at these corazones de melones
and walk over to the child who has waited
patiently with his head down the entire time
and pour water into his bowl first.
"Wow, Ms. Allie," he says,
"Look at the red! Can I play now?"
With a nod and a yes, his hands
are in the bowl making oobleck
and one by one, I pour water into the bowls
until all forty kids are happy and cheery.
I do not mind the flour on the floor
or on my face. This is a labor of love

Nymphs of the Earth

We are not like the water lilies
that do not need to think
about how to float above the pond
or lake or slow-moving stream.
They remain anchored in place
with their long stems serving
buoyancy. People travel to parks
to see them in bloom, to museums
to contemplate Monet's painting
and after four days, the lilies
let their flowers fall under the surface
to decompose in peace
without the hardened stares
of eyes that need reminding of beauty
in the era of the Anthropocene.
It is a short-lived blush and the lily pad
remains afloat, its roots imbedded
in the mud below, a resting place
for the frogs and dragonflies,
shade for the fish on a sunny day.
The lily pad continues to consume sunshine,
does not worry about its fallen flower
for it will bloom again next season.
We are not like the water lilies,
for there is a risk that if we float,
we might float away as unencumbered as clouds
and if we anchor ourselves into the ground,
we might become too snug and never rise above
past our innermost atmosphere,
and when we die, we are displayed,
surrounded by the regretful weeping
of our loved ones who have forgotten

that death comes in tandem with life
and forms into a new shape of love.

Metamorphosis

I wish I could spin myself
a chrysalis like the caterpillar
when it self-destructs
to become a butterfly,
wish I could be
just as dignified
as the caterpillar
when its tissues liquify
and its organs float freely,
repositioning themselves
as the caterpillar forms
antennae and wings.
Instead, I try my best
to keep my heart
from breaking my ribs
like wishbones
but I feel like everyone
can see me spilling out my cavity.
It happens to all of us
just before rebirth
when Shiva paves the way
and then the smoke clears
and the waters calm
and the rubble of the aftermath
is at your feet,
this broken chrysalis
from which you fly.

Love Poem

It's an awkward thing to exist,
to think about all the times
I've ever been in love or
to think about how I've drawn
mean eyes on bored faces
just to become embarrassed
by how they are staring at me.
It's a strange thing to think
about the process of unlearning
or to think about how final goodbyes
are abrupt and seldom happen.
That's why I like the passive voice,
the way its storytelling slows
the tiny moments we collect in hindsight,
compiling them into memories
like keepsake Christmas tree ornaments.
I never see things as happening to me,
the unwilling agent stuck in the underpainting.
I'm yellow like the sports car taxi cabs
changed lanes for back when my dad
was a deliveryman in the city.
I'm my mom's brute force dislodging
mortise locks, chipping paint and drywall.
On the days I would rather walk
along Flushing Avenue than ram myself
into the same glass window,
I think about home
created by the storefronts you walk into
where people know you by name.
Writings on building faces cling
onto me like an anglerfish

latching onto his love
until only the impetus remains.
The building on 49 Wyckoff Avenue says,
"Love's resilience can rebuild
bridges that were burned."
I think about the resilience of love,
how it keeps me afloat on the days
I would have liked better to drown
if it meant that I could be still,
but I know that too much momentum
is better than none at all and I know
I will get to where I'm going
by building these bridges, crossing them
and when that's done, I will return
to the earth, down south
where the dirt will keep me warm,
free of wet newspapers
that stick to pavement when it rains
and free of the spreading ink that dries
in the shape of coffee rings.
I wouldn't have to worry
about how the words disfigure
the way our plans do
when left alone to fester,
trapped like sweat bloating the body.
I can let my heart plunge
and my breathing slow
until I reach a state of torpor
beneath the frostline.

The End of the World

I am 1,600 feet above ground level wanting to jump
light-headed from the imminent fall at the precipice
that would carry my voice through the chasms
and into another's awaiting ear.
I photograph this pause and follow the path
leading back to the road. Friends and family say,
"You could have gotten lost or gripped the stone
with sweaty hands and fallen off,"
and I do wonder if my hair would have enmeshed
with the branches that look like overturned roots
or my limbs pricked with the needles of coniferous trees
before falling onto the earth made dark by dripping ice.
I used to go to church after mass just to sit and cry
underneath the arched ceiling painted in sky blue
and novenas. Stained glass windows told stories
of motherhood, sacrifice, and salvation, glowing
in a blurry but keen kind of way when I squinted.
Now, all I think about is returning
to that unleveled rock on which I stood
out of breath and satisfied, a part of the low-rolling
clouds and so perfectly alone, comforted
that I am only a fraction in the planet's many trips
around the sun, pressured to live
but not in the way that I do, gently and
bare with scabs that bleed when I pick at them,
and when I'm swallowed whole by the mouth
that has birthed me, taught me abundance by means
of a handpicked purgatory, I hope to be warm,
floating somewhere in Orion's Nebula.

Capsize

I don't think I'll be going
to space anytime soon
and will never know
what it is to be part of the dark,
my veins spilling out of its spool,
my cells the mosaic glass
that forms part of the nebulas.
The closest I'll get to it is on boat,
perhaps a canoe, floating listlessly
on the ocean's waves at twilight,
battered until the point of capsizing
with the rotting wood feeding algae.
There is only a flock of petrels
calling my name as I sink.
The sky's paint has dripped
into the sea and the sea is overspilling.
The grit on that faraway shore
is proof of the erosion.
Maybe the waves will bring
me back one day and I'll wake
with wet hair and the sun on my face.

The Figure Eight

There is magic in a woman's hips,
hips that move in figure 8s
and sashay across a room,
hips that swell with saccharine kisses,
hips that fill in space
like sacred water in a Grecian vase
that washes the Athenian man of sin
so he can approach temple.
There is magic in birthing hips
that bloom like peonies,
hips that bend and sway
like a palm tree in hurricane,
hips that beguile you with secrets,
beckoning you to come closer,
hips that lengthen spines
like serpents lifting from the grass
with flickering tongues to taste the air
for predator and prey,
hips that trap traumas
like a dream catcher's web
to make room for love,
hips as ripe as berries,
hips that fill in jeans,
dancing hips, sitting hips,
hips that move as they please.

My goodness! I love my hips!

The Language of Silence

Everyone wants to talk to the devil,
but no one wants to talk to God,
and I'm not particularly religious,
but a part of me is inquisitive
about the wind's ocean acoustics
as it tunnels through the city
vibrating the ground as we walk
or about the singing trees we gather under,
resting our backs against the bark
chatting about what's for dinner.
Surely, the trees muse about our ignorance,
the problems with our discourse
or maybe they are pleased
to be remembered at all.
If God did talk, this would be how,
by the noises our ears can pick up
when we are silent and listening
or the tremors we feel when we are still.
This is all to say, we have yet to learn
from the nature of this Earth
that we are a part of.

Daffodils

I know them by their bulbs
rounded like turnips.
They partake in a kind
of parthenogenesis,
the first to climb upright
out of cold earth and snow.
I know them by their bells,
their arctic and golden cups,
the way they recreate pockets
of sun and promise spring.
I know them by the crystals
in their sap that fissure skin
when picked and torn.
For who does not want
to consume such beauty?
Who has not fallen for the trap
that to devour is the only
way to love?

Impulses

My tía uses the internet
to find the hidden cures of the human body.
"La enfermedad señala desequilibrio," she says
and if there's one thing my tía has learned
from her hours scrolling through YouTube,
it's that our bodies are magnetic.
I guess it does make sense.
We are our own planets
pirouetting with the lunar phases,
why our sweat and tears are saline.
It is an electrical impulse that allows me
to move whenever I think to,
when a negative ion befriends a positive one.
It seems to me that Himalayan or Maldon salt
is the santo remedio to the frayed axons
of our neurons. Who knew!
"Mira!" my tía says when she sends
me the video on WhatsApp.
A man in a white lab coat cuts a bulb's wire
through the middle. He submerges the split ends
in a bowl of salt water. The lightbulb lights up
and my tía explains that our bodies
function like this too. She buys industrial magnets,
lines them in red and black fabric,
tells me to place one on my lower back
by the kidneys, another above my third eye,
and one on my chest where my heart is beating.
"Esto sanara tu cansancio," she says,
"Aclara tu mente. Relajate que no pasa nada."
I lay there with the magnets
staring at the ceiling fan and its wooden blades
until it is the only thing that exists.

A minute goes by,
ten, then thirty, an hour,
and my tía returns to collect her magnets.
I may have dozed off
but it is a little easier to lift my lids,
a little easier to sit up with my back straight.
"Ya vez," my tía says, "escucha
a los consejos de los viejos."
And I guess it does make sense.
We were all born from the ocean.

The Salt Marsh

I am enclosed in an honest cold,
sticky with blithe smog.
My bones are able to pick up
the tremble of the ocean's mouth
miles from where I stand.

When I close my eyes,
I see cattail eyelashes
frosted over and hardened.
I cry for the salt marsh,
sulfurous and misunderstood.

Keeping Symmetry

Our voices travel
        in longitudinal waves
and frolic with the other vibrations of sound.
We exist in this type of celebration
winding
        and
unwinding like an accordion
each wave changing surrounding matter.
I make a toast to water
        speak with steadfast clarity
as I pour it over the rose bushes
the areca palm
the basil and chamomile
so they are nourished
                with love
in the shape of snowflakes.
I whisper into water before I drink it
implore softly the watching eyes
of my timeline
        my mother and her laughter
                my grandfather and his gentility.
Water is the oldest traveler.
It contains the DNA
of all the living organisms
that have consumed it
                and expelled it.
It is purified with each cycle
        of its circadian rhythm

and that is why
I am fearful of the rhythm's disruption
when water is mishandled

and weaponized
        fearful of the way the oceans are tumid
with the travesties of humankind.
I hope we remember
        that we are water too
alive as moving currents in a flood
capable of cascading
        capable of drowning
that which disturbs the peace.

Ebb and Flood

If you must walk through a myriad of doors,
reluctant to look behind them,
anxious about the silent misgivings
  from me
    to you
  for me
    from you,
if you'd like to ramble along
the open stage of this chapter,
I'll let you open doors to find me.
Only then will you learn to appreciate
     the work of hinges,
  the pull between the unmoving
     and the fleeting.
You'll find meadows with orange trees
from which you can squeeze their juice,
the pink chaise lounge chair by the window
from where we watched our favorite TV shows,
and the broken promises we've written
on birthday
    and Valentine's Day cards.
When you forget that you've been searching,
teary-eyed and sated with melancholy,
I will be waiting with open arms behind a door
     to bring you to my chest,
have you careen into me like a baby clam
burrowing into the sand at the beach
during the push and pull
     of agitated tides,
and as we open our mouths to breathe
we would have learned to love the same way
sediments are shared between the ocean and shore.

An Ode to Summer

I love the feel of summer,
humid like road trips to Florida,
drowsy like a swaying hammock
at Flushing Meadows Corona Park
during a family parillada when the day
is ours and we are triumphant
in time well spent together.
I notice things that I haven't
like the smell of choclo as its grilled,
of hot dogs by the mixed caramelized nuts
served in small bags for three dollars.
I love the grease of sunscreen,
the tender wind on my bare legs,
the sweat of my thighs when I sit,
the salt on my face toward sunbursts,
and the threat of a splinter
as I walk barefoot on a boardwalk.
Only during the summer
does time slow for me.
I pretend I am a kid again
experiencing longer daylight for the first time,
surprised by the few splendid hours more
I have to contemplate the trees
with their branches heavy with leaves.
I think of the way they shimmer
like a drying watercolor painting
and I think back to when I believed
I contained that same shimmer
in my bloodstream.
At night, we see the fireflies,
hear the crack of splitting wood
at beach bonfires and campsites.

People are still out;
the night is accommodating
to the dancing on the streets.
The stars no longer
hold the responsibility of their lullaby.
I dance and I dance and I dance
and when I have burned through
all the choclo and hotdogs
and caramelized nuts,
I return home,
sleep naked in the heat until morning
and wake up to moist sheets,
my pillowcase stuck to my face.
I pretend again
that I had just survived a fever
and sweated out a nightmare.

Sea Waves and Tides

My friend tells me to find the spot
that I can hold forever
and let the minute pass.
In time, our bodies will learn to autopilot
and invite the wandering mind
to forage in the back rooms
where our most intense passions
are on the verge of violence.
She agrees with me
that grieving is eternal and so is love
and so is the bioluminescence of all living things
that comes from the breath of our cells.
It's similar to the way the larvae
of moth flies break down organic waste
in damp places like our drains.
I like these visitors on my shower walls,
the white dots on their wings
and their fuzzy bodies that remind me
of my first childhood house
when I finally had a room of my own
with sea green walls that gave me vertigo.
I tell my friend
it's not about being a beacon—
that must get lonely sometimes—
but about conserving our wonder
so we can remain happy.
I can lose myself in a spot forever,
in the smile that protects the meek,
in the stride my legs can keep for miles,
in the words written on this page
that will eventually travel onto another.
The minute will pass

and the unease will be palpable
but not a wall to break through;
there is the road
and all there is to go is forward,
but just as I'm about to leave
my friend reminds me
that it's okay to perch for a while
so we stay there in the yoga room
with the heat up to the eighties and cry
about how everything's become so green.

I'd rather not think now

would rather absorb it all to note the differences
remain confused and   root down as I search
but I am thinking
how can I exist a little less violently
together with

if it storms
beneath the pale pink of rebirth
I'll become wet   brown soil
the porous surface before the cleaving of a shovel
but I am
an artificial product of the United States of "I"

at the playground across from 3 Dollar Bill
I trace the word LOVE in the air as I did their tattoo
centered across   the skin hiding their throat
what a commitment
Are you happy
                Yes I am
Are you
        No   but I will be

Our thoughts are alive
Forty-seven percent of them   wander from us
ransack the back rooms
                that smell of recently extinguished
matches
When I close my eyes
                                I ache for the little deaths
the formlessness of clouds
enswathing Eros
imbuing space   as does time
98

which is the movement of all energy
spontaneous and entropic
                  the humming of a dial tone

Finding My Route Home

My mother hated turning corners at night.
"Allí se esconden los ladrones," she'd say,
whispering in my ear as we'd approach one,
"Camina donde hay luz y anda con cuidado."
We would take the most direct route home
alongside busy roads crammed with red taillights.
For a long time, my legs only knew how to trample
over dried leaves and stomp in puddles
wearing chancletas that were too big for me
and I'd curl my toes to keep them on,
their soles slinging mud behind my ankles.
I eventually learned how to walk and then run for miles
by taking in gulps of air to inflate myself like a balloon.
I appreciate the fullness of expansionary things—
eggs, pregnancy, words, and the heavenly light
guiding me on my walks at night and before daybreak.
Sometimes, when I'm alone, shadows morph
into nondescript figures and the lampposts
make the concrete glint wet after the downpour
of heavy rain in the ephemeral obscurity.
It is almost as if I am swimming underwater
and the pressure in my ears reminds me
 of my physical body, a body that can disappear
into the transient landscape or disappear
indefinitely never to be found again.
I am nearing the next corner and my mother
is no longer here to remind me to walk slowly
underneath illuminated store signs, so I listen
to the ache in my legs and sprint down the block
in my orange sneakers. I inhale for a count of four
and when the day does break, black revealing
changing blues that give way to pink and gold,

I will be somewhere else
and maybe in all the sun touches
simply filling up space as a way of existing.

Acknowledgements

[1] Conversations with the Buoy: Homage to Frank M. Charles Memorial Park in Howard Beach.

[2] Shipwreck and an Hourglass: Inspired by Jean-Dominique Bauby's *The Diving Bell and the Butterfly*. (Translated by Jeremy Leggatt, Vintage Books, 1998)

[3] A Lone Canoe in the Living Room: "I should buy a canoe...it is time." Inspired by Nathaniel Rich's *Odds Against Tomorrow: A Novel.* (Picador, 2014)

[4] Lo Real Maravilloso: "Lo real maravilloso." Term coined by Alejo Carpentier in the prologue of *The Kingdom of this World*. (1949)

[5] Lo Real Maravilloso: "the foodbearing...Pleiades." Refers to the Amerindian legend of the foodbearing tree.

[6] Circles: "Intra-action." Term coined by Karen Barad in *Meeting the Universe Halfway* (Duke University Press, 2007) 33.

[7] Circles: "an atom collided...boom!." Inspired by a line in Clarice Lispector's *The Hour of the Star* that states "One molecules said yes to another molecule and life was born." Translated by Benjamin Moser. (New Directions, 2011) 3.

[8] The Greener Grass: Mentions *The Kingdom of this World*. (Personal copy, Farrar Straus Giroux, 1989)

[9] The Vortex: "but consciousness...choices." Marianne Szegedy-Maszak, "Mysteries of the Mind" (*U.S. News*, 2005):

[10] Sea Waves and Tides: "forage in the backrooms..." Inspired by Carmen Martín-Gaite's *The Back Room* (City Lights Publishers, 2001).

^{11.} I'd rather not think right now: "how can...violently." Inspired by a line in Donna Haraway's *The Companion Species Manifesto: Dogs, People, and Significant Otherness* that states "...worldly actors might somehow be accountable to and love each other less violently." (Prickly Paradigm Press, 2003) 7.

^{12.} I'd rather not think right now: "together with." Inspired by the term "sympoiesis" coined by Donna Haraway in *Staying with the Trouble: Making Kin in the Chthulucene* (Duke University Press, 2016) 58.

^{13.} I'd rather not think right now: "Forty-seven percent of them/wander from us." Killingsworth, M. A., and D. T. Gilbert. "A Wandering Mind Is an Unhappy Mind." (2010) doi:10.1126/science.1192439.

^{14.} I'd rather not think right now: "ransack the...matches." Inspired by Carmen Martín-Gaite's *The Back Room* (City Lights Publishers, 2001).

About the Author

Ashley 'Allie' Iliana Herrera was born and raised in Queens, first along Jamaica Avenue before moving to Woodhaven along the same strip. She moved to Bushwick after graduating with a BA degree in English and World Literature and Creative Writing from Marymount Manhattan College. She now calls Bushwick her forever home and spends most of her time in the neighborhood. Allie has previously worked as a local journalist for Bushwick Daily and freelanced with BK Reader. Most recently, she was a local afterschool Creative Writing Teaching Artist. You can find Allie at a coffee shop writing or reading, hiking in upstate New York, or in Queens with her family where she often takes her dogs, Kim Nana Pelusa and Chichi Beriberi Ruby on walks to Forest Park. You can visit Allie's website at theantsyverse.com or follow them on Instagram @allieihg.